All Tutus Should Be *Pink*

For Barbara, of course,
with a hug for Emilie.
—S.B.

Text copyright © 1992 by Sheri Brownrigg.
Illustrations copyright © 1992 by Meredith Johnson.

Library of Congress Cataloging-in-Publication Data is available.

ISBN-13: 978-0-590-43904-6
ISBN-10: 0-590-43904-9

20 19   10 11 12 13 14/0

Printed in the U.S.A. 40 • This edition first printing, May 2008

All Tutus
Should Be

DEVELOPING READER
LEVEL
2
250-750 WORDS

Pink

by Sheri Brownrigg
Illustrated by Meredith Johnson

Cartwheel
·B·O·O·K·S·®

SCHOLASTIC INC.

New York Toronto London Auckland Sydney
Mexico City New Delhi Hong Kong Buenos Aires

I love my new tutu!

It's pink.

I had another pink tutu,
but it got too small for me.

My dog Pepe-Pierre
wears it now.

Emily has a pink tutu, too.

She's the best friend
I ever had.

We wear our tutus everywhere.

To the grocery store.

To the movies.

Even to the beach.

The real reason
we have our tutus
is dance class.

Our favorite person is
our dance teacher,
Ms. Yvonne.

She used to be a famous
pink tutu dancer.

We know this because
there are pictures of her
at the studio.

We want to grow up to be famous pink tutu dancers, too.

But I think we
would wear our tutus
even if we were
truck drivers!

Dance class looks like fun,
but it is hard.

Sometimes it's so hard,
Emily thinks she might faint.
And we want to quit.

Then we look at ourselves
in the mirror and see how
great we look.

And we keep on dancing.

Tutus make a magic *swoosh* sound
every time we move.

Sometimes we move a little extra
to make extra *swooshes*.

Others in class
wear their tutus
only on stage.

For Emily and me,
all the world is a stage.

After dance class
we are so famished!

We need to eat ice cream.
Strawberry only, please!

If we drop some on our tutus,
it doesn't matter.

They're pink, too.

That's why
all tutus should be pink.
I love my new tutu!